W9-CED-499

Calvert *the* Raven *in* *The* Battle *of* Baltimore

Written & Illustrated by **J. Scott Fuqua**

Brought to you by Historyworks, Inc., Baltimore, MD
www.historyworks-inc.com

Additional materials, for students and teachers alike, available at www.bancroftpress.com.

Copyright 2012 by Jonathon Scott Fuqua
All rights reserved.

No part of this book may be reproduced in any form or by electronic means,
including information storage and retrieval systems, without written permission from the publisher,
except by a reviewer, who may quote passages in a review.

All the characters in this book are fictitious, and any resemblance to actual persons, living or dead, is purely coincidental.

Cover Design by Susan Mangan
Book Design by Susan Mangan
Author Photo by Calla Fuqua

Library of Congress Control Number: 2012944778
ISBN 978-1-61088-077-0 (cloth)
ISBN 978-1-61088-078-7 (paperback)
ISBN 978-1-61088-079-4 (mobi)
ISBN 978-1-61088-080-0 (epub)

First Edition
Printed in the United States of America

bancroft press

Published by Bancroft Press ("Books that enlighten")
P.O. Box 65360, Baltimore, MD 21209
410-358-0658 (phone)
410-764-1967 (fax)
www.bancroftpress.com

aniel searched up through the bright Baltimore sky, where a raven curled in front of the sun. He lowered his gaze to the wrinkled history paper in his hand and reread the first paragraph:

> When you look back at the War of 1812, you wondor a lot of things. You wondor why somebuddy didn't invent the camera yet so that you could see real pictures of everyone insted of paintings. And, you think everything seems a little boaring. Stories about back then put me asleep in about five seconds. So, on account of being scared of going asleep, I couldn't not even open a book. If I could, I couldn't of written this essay. That's why I had to make so many things up. It's true.

At the top of the page, his teacher had written in cursive letters, "Terrible!"

Daniel worried that his mom and dad would be furious when they saw the paper. They might even take away TV or the computer for a whole entire week, which would be like being starved for fun.

Above Daniel, the raven cawed, extra loud. Then, like a well-made paper airplane, it circled downward and skittered onto the bench beside him.

Daniel looked at it. "Hey," he said. "You're a friendly bird, aren't you?"

"Yeah," it said.

Daniel stumbled backwards like he was pushed. He scatched an itchy nostril. "Ah, you didn't just talk . . . did you?"

"Yeah."

Daniel leaned toward the bird, eyeballing him suspiciously. "But . . . birds can't talk."

"How about parrots? You remember those, Einstein?"

"Oh," Daniel mumbled. "Well . . . you're not a parrot, are you?"

"I'm a raven."

"A raven? Like the football team?"

The bird cleared his throat. "Like the bird. Name's Calvert."

"Calvert?"

"Yup."

"You've sorta been following me since school. I've seen you."

"That's not a crime, is it?"

Daniel considered. "I . . . I don't think. Not for a bird."

"Good. Wouldn't want to commit another one of those."

Daniel stepped closer. He whispered, "Another? Are you a criminal?"

"Not me. It's that sorry history paper that's criminal. Ouch."

Self-conscious, Daniel hid the paper behind his back. "It's a boring subject."

The raven jumped from the seat to the back of the bench. "Ya really think it's boring?"

Daniel didn't know how to answer.

"Tell me something. Do ya think life and death is boring?"

Daniel put a finger to his chin. "No."

"Are bombs and rockets a yawner?"

"No."

"Can I try to change your mind about the war?"

"Some, yeah," Daniel said.

Calvert leaped up like someone had poked his tail feathers. "This could take a while, but ya won't be late for dinner. I promise."

"What could take a while?"

"Me changing your mind. We gotta go on a trip."

"I'm not allowed to go places with strangers."

"Daniel, please, I'm not a stranger. I'm a bird."

Daniel thought for a minute. "It's true. My parents never said anything about you guys."

"That's what I thought. Touch my wing. Just for a second."

Nervous, Daniel put a pinky forward and pressed it on a dark, slick feather.

Suddenly, a gust of wind swept his hair back. His stomach knotted. He looked down and realized he wasn't on the sidewalk anymore.

Somehow, he was sitting atop Calvert as the raven whisked him above an old-fashioned sailing ship.

Calvert adjusted his wings and dropped down amidst a pack of similar ships, all of them bristling with cannons and men.

Daniel shouted, "How . . . how is this happening?!"

"What?"

"Me being here?!"

"I brought you."

"How?!"

Calvert looked over his shoulder at Daniel. "How do ya ride a bike, dude? I don't know how I did it."

Daniel shouted, over the wind whistling in his ears, "Have we gone back in time?!"

"Yup."

"Did you make yourself gigantic? Is that how I can fit on your back?"

"Of course not. I can't do that. I made you small."

Daniel's head whirled like he was getting spun in tight circles. "O-oh," he stammered.

Calvert veered gently, gained altitude, and glided toward a distant point of land, and before it, more tall ships. They rested at anchor, their sails pulled up. The bird said, "See those buildings and houses way, way over there?"

Daniel blinked. "Yeah."

"That's Baltimore in 1814."

"That little town?"

"I ain't lying. And it's the third biggest city in all of America. Later this morning, British soldiers will attack the American army outside of Baltimore. They're the same soldiers who charbroiled Washington, D.C., the White House, and the Capitol Building a month ago."

Daniel hollered, "They didn't char-cook the real White House, did they?!"

"President had to run away and hide, like a mouse from a cat."

"Is . . . is that weird?"

"It is to me, yeah."

Calvert glided over the ships anchored by the coastline. "Over the next few days, Daniel, the United States might get beaten. It's a sad situation."

Daniel peered down at the ranks of soldiers on the shoreline below them. "I . . . I hope those are Americans," he said nervously.

"They aren't. They're British Redcoats marching to capture Baltimore."

Shocked, Daniel said, "But America won't lose. Right?"

"Don't know. History is watery. It goes where it wants. Just us being here could change everything. For instance, what if you and me distract someone from doing something they were supposed to do? We could change the way history happens, and America might lose the war."

Far below, hidden by trees, Daniel heard the distant sound of trumpets and drums. Then, like a thunderstorm, cannons roared and muskets whooshed. "What's happening?!" he yelled.

"It's the Battle of North Point!" Calvert hollered, looping sideways and plummeting down between sharp tree branches before rocketing above a field where two armies were pounding away at one another. Cannons thundered. Lines of men shot at other lines of men. The Americans wore mostly blue. The British wore mostly red.

Calvert and Daniel torpedoed through the American positions. A musket ball sizzled over their heads. "Oh geez," Calvert muttered.

Everywhere, clouds of smoke curled like brownish-blue fog. A cabin burned like newspaper. Men shouted and fell.

It was terrifying.

Then lines of British soldiers rushed forward. Americans fired back. Men perspired. Boys loaded rifles. Dogs barked.

The fight went on for hours. Daniel was both horrified and fascinated. He didn't sense the passing of time. He didn't notice the movement of the sun or the shadows on the ground growing longer.

The British pushed so close to the American troops that they could throw sticks at each other. Breezes tore at the smoke so that it looked like cloth.

"We're losing!" Daniel said. "How can we lose?"

Calvert said, "Somebody always does."

Eventually, American soldiers carefully moved backwards, firing as they disappeared into the trees.

British soliders, breathing hard, didn't chase after the Americans. They were tired. Men from both sides had died.

"Don't look at the battlefield," said Calvert. "It's an awful sight—a terrible sight." A soft rain started falling. "War is a sorry thing to see," Calvert said. "It's just a sorry, sad scene, huh?"

Daniel nodded, but his voice didn't work. He felt too many things all at once.

Calvert gained speed and swerved amongst trees and falling leaves before settling on a branch. Below, American soldiers stumbled into camps, dragging their guns and their packs, dirt covering their white pants and blood oozing from their knuckles. They lit fires, cooked food, and sang sad songs.

Gloomy, Daniel asked, "Are you sure I'm ever going home?"

Calvert looked up at him. "Of course ya will. I wouldn't kidnap ya. I said I'd get ya home before dinner, and unless we get hit by something, I will."

"But it's turning into nighttime."

"Here it is, but not in the future."

To Daniel, that idea was hard to understand.

Darkness came and rain fell, sometimes hard and sometimes soft. Daniel listened to the soldiers talk and sing softly. "I'm going to have nightmares," he mumbled, "forever."

"You'll be eating pizza with your family soon enough," Calvert said. "This'll be a memory, and you'll be the same lazy kid ya always were. I promise, Daniel."

After a minute, Daniel said, "Oh."

An hour later, Daniel was asleep and dreaming about clouds of smoke and men being brave. Eight hours after that, he awoke, damp and cold in the darkness just before dawn.

Seated on a branch high above, Daniel and Calvert watched the American troops, organized in trenches and ditches facing the British army.

A distant boom shook Daniel's wet hair. More booms followed.

Daniel asked, "What's that?"

"That, my friend, is the bombardment of Fort McHenry," Calvert said. "Ya remember the fleet of sailing ships splashing their way toward Baltimore yesterday? The British are firing on the fort. Worse, Daniel, our cannons in the fort can't even reach the Britsh ships. They aren't strong enough. Fort McHenry has to take the punishment and can't even fight back."

Calvert jumped into the air, swept down, and grabbed a biscuit from a startled soldier's plate. "Got us some breakfast," he told Daniel as he gained altitude and took the biscuit up in his beak. He craned his neck and gave it to Daniel. Daniel broke it in half and gave a piece back to Calvert.

As Calvert and Daniel ate, they rose above the trees toward the gray, cloud-covered sky.

In the distance, bombs continued exploding above the fort. Calvert banked and carried Daniel slowly toward the action, past little settlements and buildings and across the shiny waterway.

When they were high above the fleet of warships, Calvert finished his breakfast, then suddenly tucked his wings and dropped like a meteor.

Daniel screamed, the remainder of his biscuit flying from his hands.

"AHHHHHHHHHHHHHHHHHHHHHHHHHHH!!!!!!!!"
His full stomach rose up into his throat.

"Don't be such a chicken!" Calvert shouted.

"But . . . we're . . . gonna . . . die!"

"Not even," Calvert said. A car-length above the water, he pulled up, zipping between two ships and beneath the bow of a third. Adjusting, Calvert aimed for the fort.

"Don't ever do that again!" Daniel hollered, his eyes the size of baseballs.

"Toughen up, my friend," Calvert said with a snicker.

Cannons bellowed behind them.

"Oh, great," Daniel said. "Now we're gonna get shot in the back!" He peeked over his shoulder.

"Fraidy-cat," Calvert said, darting above the waves like a seagull. Halfway to the fort, he jerked sideways to avoid a fragment of hot orange metal whizzing by them. "Wow, that woulda hurt," he mumbled just loud enough for Daniel to hear.

Just past the shoreline, they glided over American soldiers hiding behind trenches and barricades. Calvert said, "See? They won't even try shooting at the British. Their cannons won't go that far. It's sorta unfair, huh?"

"It's like at school when some big kid picks on you and you know you can't do anything about it."

"Sorta, yeah. Except they don't have cannons."

"I might go crazy out here," said Daniel.

"Some will," Calvert said. "That's the sad part."

The two skimmed over the fort's brick walls and between small buildings. They passed by the flagpole with the stars and stripes snapping like a whip in the rain. Banking, they whistled past a courtyard as exploding metal slapped against the ground and the wooden rooftops.

Eventually, Calvert carried them above the action, dipping and darting between exploding rockets like they were harmless leaves falling from unseen branches.

With all of the excitement and drama, the afternoon came quickly.

Daniel said, "We're gonna lose, aren't we? I'm worried we're gonna lose."

Calvert said, "Major Armistead, the officer defending the fort, won't surrender, Daniel. Unless they're completely flattened."

"I would."

"No ya wouldn't. You're a lot stronger than you know."

Eventually, Calvert peeled away and headed toward the woods where they'd slept the night before. The bombardment of Fort McHenry faded behind them, replaced by the shouts of men and the distant sounds of muskets popping.

"People are fighting all over," Daniel said, amazed.

"We're in the thick of the Battle of Baltimore. It'll determine America's future. That's your future. Who knows, Daniel? When I deliver ya back home, the country of America might not exist anymore."

"Really?"

"Really, dude."

Daniel wondered if he'd suddenly have an accent like Harry Potter from the movies. He thought he might like that part of being British—but only that part. No other parts would be any good. Especially because he liked being American. He understood what being an American meant now.

"Look over there," Calvert said as they approached the shore. He lifted a wing and indicated a hilltop. "Those two men are the American commanders. Major General Samuel Smith, the man who prepared the city for battle, has the silver hair, while the other is Commodore John Rodgers. Now they're trying to guess what the British army will do so that they can counter it, like a giant chess match. They're brilliant men, Daniel, real heroes."

They soared above America's lines. "Commodore Rodgers, Daniel, was sent out by the government to attack the ships of countries we're fighting. He captained a ship called the USS *President* and captured twenty-three British ships. Twenty-three."

"That's pretty good, huh?"

"Pretty good? Daniel, that's great."

"Wow. Wow, huh, Calvert?"

"Yup. Wow."

Calvert swooped over the battle. Once more, heavy clouds of gunpowder boiled from the trenches. The sound of muskets echoed. Cannons roared. The British probed one section of the battlefield after another. As the day wore on, the Redcoats gathered in front of the American fortifications as if preparing for a huge, frightening charge. But they didn't rush forward.

"What're they doing?" Daniel asked.

"Looks like they might be giving up."

"I hope. Do you?"

Calvert nodded. "Oh, yeah, I do. I sorta like America."

Time passed. Eventually, the Redcoats retreated to their camps. Many of them limped, most stumbled, and a few were carried.

"They quit!" Daniel shouted. "You see? You see how they quit?"

"They're worn out, is all," Calvert said.

Daniel nodded. He was worn out, too. He shivered from the rain and worried, silently, out of nowhere, that he'd never see his parents or even his crummy brother again. He felt homesick. "Is it over now?" he asked.

"I don't know," Calvert said. "We need a place to watch this mess."

In the growing darkness, Calvert rose steeply, higher and higher. Then he coasted back toward the bay, like a bike rolling down a long hill. They whisked over rough salty water and gray waves. Behind them, bright rockets glittered in the sky, lighting up the fort.

Calvert and Daniel approached the ships at anchor, their wooden masts and hulls creaking like an old house in the night.

Calvert landed amongst the ropes and rigging of a giant, ancient warship anchored amidst the others. Standing on a thick, tight rope, the raven tiptoed sideways until he stood beneath the maintop, out of the rain. "I know it's been a long day for ya, Daniel, but for the men in the fort, it's been even longer."

Daniel lowered his head and watched the continuing bombardment of Fort McHenry.

"The way it's stuck out on that point of land," Daniel said, "it looks like the whole fort could sink."

"It kinda does," Calvert said.

Throughout the night, Daniel worried about going home to his room and his warm bed and his cat Marcel. He worried, too, about Fort McHenry—that in the morning, Fort McHenry might look like a collapsed sandcastle.

The rain continued falling. "Please," Daniel whispered to himself. "Please let everything be okay."

In time, the eastern horizon brightened. Just before dawn, Calvert twitched his feathers.

Daniel, his hair flattened to his head, yawned and squinted.

Bombs continued to explode above the faraway shoreline.

Calvert said, "Look down there, Daniel. What do you see?"

Daniel searched through the ropes and rigging. "Sunrise," he said.

"No, standing on the smaller ship right there."

Daniel rose up on the bird's back and spotted a man lifting a telescope to an eye. "There's a man looking through a spyglass. There's also a person behind him."

Suddenly, it grew quiet. The bombardment had stopped. "That's right," Calvert said. "Do you know who he is?"

"Ah . . . no."

"Ya serious, boy?" Calvert laughed.

Daniel shrugged. "Is he an admiral?"

"Course he isn't. He's not wearing a uniform."

"Is he the president?"

"Ya really didn't read your history, did ya? The guy's Francis Scott Key. Do ya recognize the name?"

"Did he invent the car?"

Calvert winced as if he'd dropped something on a toe. "Ah, no, Daniel. He will write a song called 'Defence of Fort McHenry,' which will eventually become 'The Star-Spangled Banner,' our national anthem. At this very moment, Mr. Francis Scott Key is looking to see if our flag is still there. I suppose it might not be this time."

Daniel gazed downward and watched Mr. Key. A slow, slow minute passed. The man lowered the spyglass and stared distantly.

Daniel grew sure that something terrible had occurred because Mr. Key appeared so serious, so silent. Then Mr. Key turned to the man behind him. Grinning, he suddenly shouted, "It's still there! Somehow, the flag is still there!"

Calvert exhaled.

So did Daniel. Silent and even a little nervous, he stared out across the water and spotted, far, far away, the American flag flapping like a sheet on a clothesline.

"Well, well, well," Calvert said. "Now, if all follows form, the British army will be marching back toward its ships in order to leave Maryland for good. And within the hour, these warships will turn tail and sail for the Chesapeake Bay, never to return."

"I can't believe it!" Daniel whispered. "America won!"

"Guess we didn't do any harm or change any history, huh?" Calvert said.

"Guess you're right," Daniel said, grinning.

Calvert turned his head to eyeball Daniel. "Now, how 'bout I get ya home for dinner?"

"But I kinda wanna see the celebrations now."

"But ya have to go. You've seen what I wanted ya to see, Einstein."

Then, suddenly, Daniel was standing on the sidewalk by the road near his school. The sunlight made him blink. He stumbled backwards, caught his heel on a crack, and landed on his rear end.

Calvert jumped out of the way. "Darn if ya didn't nearly fall on me," the raven said.

Daniel looked at Calvert. "Sorry."

"No worries. You're a little tired, I guess."

"Yeah."

"Is it two days later?"

"It's a minute later. That's all."

"But . . ." Daniel said. "How?"

"Daniel, please, I know what I'm doing—least I do sometimes." The bird, with his large dark beak, appeared to smile.

"Calvert," Daniel said, "that was the most amazing thing I've ever done."

"Of course it was." Calvert stepped backwards and adjusted his wings. "Now, my friend, please go rewrite that criminally bad paper of yours, even if your teacher doesn't change your grade. It's an insult to the people of Baltimore."

"It all feels like a dream."

"But it wasn't, Daniel."

Daniel watched the bird turn and amble away. He called after him, "I won't be so surprised when you talk next time!"

"I hope not," Calvert said.

"Calvert," Daniel said, "are we friends now?"

"Of course we are. Daniel, you're a smart boy. Ya don't even know how smart ya are. I just want ya to think before ya decide not to care about things."

"I'm gonna try," Daniel whispered.

"Good," Calvert said. He leaped into the air. Like a dark firework, the raven zipped upwards. Overhead, he circled once, waved the tip of a pen feather, and disappeared behind swaying treetops.

Daniel smiled. He felt funny. He was both sad and happy. His stomach, beneath his belt, rumbled like a distant cannon. He was nearly starved. Excited to see his family, to tell them about the war and Commodore John Rodgers, he ran down the old—but not so old—Baltimore sidewalk for home, his head filled with memories of brave men and tattered flags and a raven that could talk like a parrot, only better.